T0197486

Politics 4 Kids
Think 4 Change

Written & Created
By
Michael J. Falcaro

The next generation of any era has a chance to make a change. You can make a difference by engaging to make your actions louder than words…

The World is divided. It's not your fault. Many adults stop talking to each other over opinions. Opinions can make anyone narrow minded if we stop caring about opinions outside our own. Politics has a lot to do with opinions. It's up to us to navigate opinions and politics to change the world for the better. "Opinion has caused more trouble on this little Earth than plagues or earthquakes." ~ Voltaire

Kids on the other hand are naturally open minded. It is up to you to stay that way. It is great to be passionate. In fact, the first step to save the world is to care about it. When we stop caring about the world or each other, people separate. "The greatest danger to our future is apathy." ~ Dr. Jane Goodall

Adults will often say not to talk about politics; it doesn't mean politics are bad. Politics is how people make agreements and compromises while making decisions that can impact all of us. Politics also plays a big part in deciding what groups to belong to, either be a social club, tribe, city or country. "Politics is not a game, but a serious business." ~ Winston Churchill

The more popular a person or idea becomes, the more powerful it becomes. Politics end up being pushed onto everyone, everywhere in many examples from neighbors debating beliefs, imaginary lines on a map, shows we watch, or books we read. "Be a free thinker and don't accept everything you hear as truth. Be critical and evaluate what you believe in." ~ Aristotle

Some people will try to make you think like they do and instead of having a healthy debate, they will blame everyone but themselves even if they are wrong. "You have the power over your mind, not outside events. Realize this and you will find strength." ~ Marcus Aurelius

Politicians are public servants; which means, they work for us and are supposed to make good decisions for all of us. That's why we vote for them; which is also why many adults get upset when whomever they vote for doesn't win. "The Human Being is a political animal." ~Aristotle

Being popular in politics can make you powerful. Power can make people forget what is important and think only about themselves. The history of the world has shown mans' desire for power to never be satisfied. "It is of the nature of desire not to be satisfied, and most men live only for the gratification of it." ~ Aristotle

Patriotism is supporting your country all the time and your government when it deserves it"~ Mark Twain

Divided States of America

Partisanship is Poison

7

Sometimes politicians and businesses divide people over issues that keep everyone distracted for selfish reasons. "Politics have no relation to morals." ~ Niccolo Machiavelli

Throughout history we have witnessed mean behaviors like sexisism, racism and selfish acts. All you need to do is care about the world so these bad things cease to exist. "If you do not take interest in the affairs of your Government, then you are doomed to live under the rule of fools." ~ Plato

Some adults might say kids are disrespectful but in turn disrespect other adults through their inability to consider other opinions. If you (yourself) become divided with others, go easy on yourself. Almost all our behavior is learned behavior. You are responsible for your own actions but sometimes we repeat things said or seen. We can't control what we see or hear but we can control what we (ourselves) say and do. "It is easier to build strong children than to repair broken men." ~ Frederick Douglas

No matter what, you can reset yourself each moment of your life to start over. We are all flawed and make mistakes. If your guardian makes mistakes, go easy on them, just like you would yourself. The world needs us to start over sometimes. "How wonderful is it that nobody need a single moment before starting to improve the World." ~ Anne Frank

Instead of working together and focusing on our common humanity, adults sometimes judge one another poorly over who they like, love, believe in or even if they wave a different flag. Only you can decide what's important to you, but in doing so, please know that peace starts with empathy. Empathy puts yourself in another's situation, perspectives, and so much more. "I think we all have empathy. We may not all have the courage to display it." ~ Maya Angelou

Leading with empathy is great because you take time to understand others' backgrounds, beliefs, culture, morals, and views that may differ from your own. It can be difficult to slow down and take the time to hear or see other perspectives, especially when they are not something we agree with; however, everyone is worth the effort of empathy. "Empathy is the medicine the world needs." ~ Dr. Judith Orloff

Generations before you have really divided things. People have grown so far apart on issues and have lost focus on what's really important; which is each other. "Our differences do matter but our common humanity matters more." ~ Bill Clinton

Making the world a better place is a task we all need to take part in. It's not something that can be done alone. "There is no limit to the amount of good that can be done, if you don't care who gets the credit." ~ Ronald Reagan

Today can be better than yesterday and tomorrow can be better than today. What's the point of anything if we stop trying to make the world better? Politics are most powerful where they begin; which is with each individual. That makes you more powerful than you know. Don't let others cause divide. The world depends on you to care enough about it, to make it better. "Change will not come if we wait for some other person or some other time. We are the ones we've been waiting for. We are the change we seek." ~ Barack Obama

Aside from keeping an open mind, leading with empathy and learning from mistakes made by others, you can arm yourself with education. When people think they know it all, it just shows how much more they need to learn. Educating ourselves is a never ending journey. Change comes from knowledge. "Education is the most powerful weapon which can be used to change the World." Nelson Mandela

With knowledge and empathy, kids have the power to change the world. If you work hard and care enough, you can change the World. "Be the Change you want to see in the world." ~ Mahatma Gandhi

Change starts with you.

To order additional copies of this book, contact:
Xlibris
844-714-8691
www.Xlibris.com
Orders@Xlibris.com

ISBN: Softcover   978-1-6698-1566-2
         EBook   978-1-6698-1565-5

Print information available on the last page

Rev. date: 04/13/2022

Printed in the United States
by Baker & Taylor Publisher Services